# THE QUEST
# FOR THE ALLSPARK

Transformers: The Quest for the Allspark
Printed in the United States of America.
For information address HarperCollins Children's Books,
a division of HarperCollins Publishers,
1350 Avenue of the Americas, New York, NY 10019.
www.harpercollinschildrens.com

Library of Congress catalog card number: 2006935095
ISBN-13: 978-0-06-088834-3 — ISBN-10: 0-06-088834-2

❖

First Edition

# TRANSFORMERS™

# THE QUEST
# FOR THE ALLSPARK

Adapted by Annie Auerbach

HarperEntertainment
*An Imprint of HarperCollinsPublishers*

# PROLOGUE

In the far reaches of space, Cybertron was once a thriving planet, home to an alien race called the Transformers. Most revered among them were Optimus and Megatron. They were twin brothers of the Prime dynasty.

But greed overtook Megatron, and soon he sought power and control. Turning against his brother, Megatron built up an army called the Decepticons—they were known for their deceit. Ruthless and aggressive, these evil Transformers were bent on destruction. They had unique qualities, perfect for warring against Optimus's army, the Autobots. Starscream, Bonecrusher, Brawl, Barricade, Skorponok, Blackout, and Frenzy followed Megatron into battle.

The Decepticons unleashed a war so violent that Cybertron was left in ruin. The Transformer race was nearly extinguished, and those who survived were forced to flee the planet in search of the Allspark—the only remaining source of the Transformers' life force. If the Autobots could find the Allspark, they could return to their home and

1

rebuild their race. Optimus, along with his fellow Autobots, Bumblebee, Jazz, Ironhide, and Ratchet, followed the Decepticons to another planet, far off in the galaxy, where the battle of good versus evil would continue. That planet was . . . Earth.

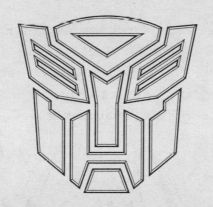

# CHAPTER ONE

I n 1897, deep in the Arctic Circle, an expedition crew was in trouble. Axes rose and fell as the men worked desperately to try and free their ship from the blocks of ice surrounding it.

"Put your backs into it, or we'll be chopping our way back to the States!" ordered Captain Witwicky.

Just then, their pack of huskies began to howl at something off in the distance.

"There's something out there," a sailor said, as the dogs took off.

The captain grabbed his rifle and lantern. He and two other men carefully made their way to a large floe, where the dogs pawed at the ice.

MEGATRON

"Whatever it is, it's below the ice," said one of the men.

"*Nothing's* alive below this ice," the captain replied.

Suddenly a huge rift opened. The men dived to safety, but one of the dogs fell through the giant crack. As the captain grabbed for the husky, he fell into a thirty-foot-deep ravine. Down they tumbled, landing hard on something. Dazed, the captain made sure the dog was all right and then got his bearings.

"I'm okay, lads!" he shouted to his worried crewmen.

Captain Witwicky looked around and was surprised to find that he was standing on the palm of a giant steel hand, half submerged in the ice. Embedded within the ice wall was a mechanical face—its expression frozen in a scream. Shock and confusion washed over the captain. Then he saw an unrecognizable symbol on the mechanoid. Curious, he pulled out his pickax.

*Whack! Whack!*

The ice cracked . . . triggering something on the mechanoid's body. A laser blast shot out from the metal and burned the captain's eyes.

"*Aahhhh!*" screamed Captain Witwicky, collapsing to the ground, covering his eyes. His glasses

went flying off his head and hit the ground with a *crack.*

"Captain? Captain?!" yelled the men from the top of the ravine.

Trembling, Captain Witwicky searched for his glasses. He put them on, but it was no use. He was blind.

# CHAPTER TWO

Over a century later, the captain's great-great-grandson sat in his eleventh-grade classroom. Sam Witwicky was a typical seventeen-year-old—one who dreamed about getting a car and getting the popular girl in class. For him, that girl was Mikaela Banes. Unfortunately, Mikaela already had a boyfriend. But this didn't keep Sam from staring . . . or hoping.

Sam was daydreaming of Mikaela when he heard his teacher's voice. "Okay, Sam, you're up," Mr. Hosney said.

Sam rose from his seat, grabbed his backpack, and headed to the front of the class.

"Um, so," he began, "for my family genealogy report, I picked my great-great-grandfather Captain Archibald Witwicky, one of the first guys ever to make it to the Arctic Circle." He opened his backpack and laid out his great-great-grandfather's navigation instruments, including his glasses.

"This isn't show-and-tell, Mr. Witwicky," Mr. Hosney said.

"Yeah, I know," replied Sam. "It's just that I'm also selling this stuff on eBay to put toward my car fund—"

"Sam . . ."

"Right," said Sam. "Anyway, I guess years of hypothermia froze his brain, and he ended up going blind and crazy in a sanitarium, drawing these weird symbols and babbling about a giant ice man." He held up a faded newspaper clipping that read ARCTIC ADVENTURER ALLEGES ICE MAN FOUND.

Just then the bell rang, and the kids filed out the door.

"So what's my grade?" Sam asked Mr. Hosney.

"I'd say a solid B minus," replied the teacher.

Sam panicked. "When I turned sixteen last year, my dad said that if I saved two thousand bucks and got three As, he'd help me buy half a car. I need at least an A minus," Sam pleaded. "Please, Mr. Hosney. My future, my freedom—my *manhood*—is

in your merciful hands."

Mr. Hosney raised an eyebrow and considered the situation.

Outside, Ron Witwicky waited for his son. When Sam got in the car, he looked glum.

"So?" asked his father.

Sam turned to his dad and grinned. "You owe me a car, Pops."

\* \* \*

A little while later, Ron pulled into a used-car lot.

"Here?" asked Sam. "No, no, no, Dad. There's a food chain in high school, and it's not that I'm on the bottom. I'm not even on it." Sam had hoped a cool car would get him in with the popular crowd, and this was *not* the place to get anything cool. Unfortunately, his father had other ideas.

As Sam looked around, all he saw was one hunk of junk after another. Suddenly he spotted a 1975 yellow Camaro. Sam circled the car, tracing a finger along the black racing stripes.

The used-car salesman stared at the car. "Where'd this one come from?" he said, confused.

Sam hopped in. A glint of light on the steering wheel caught his eye. He wiped away the grime to reveal an emblem: the Autobot symbol. Sam wondered what it meant.

"How much?" Ron asked the salesman.

"Well, uh, considering the semiclassic nature of the vehicle, five grand," said the salesman.

"We're not going above four," Ron told him.

"Four? Kid, get out of the car," said the salesman. He tried to show Sam another car, but the Camaro's passenger door swung open and hit it. When the salesman shut the Camaro door, its horn blared so loud that the windows in all the other cars shattered!

Desperate to get rid of the strange car, the salesman changed his offer to Sam and Ron. "It's your lucky day! On account of the kinks, four thousand."

Sam looked at his dad with hopeful eyes. Finally, Ron nodded.

*"Yes!"* cheered Sam. He got into the Camaro and peeled out of the lot. Little did he know that he was in for the ride of his life.

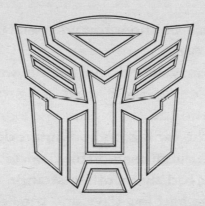

# CHAPTER THREE

Far from high schools and used-car lots, Air Force One soared through the sky. On board, the president was hard at work.

In a nearby cabin, a boom box suddenly came to life. It sprouted tiny feet and transformed into a four-and-a-half-foot-tall Decepticon called Frenzy.

Unnoticed by the Secret Service agents, Frenzy scuttled around until he finally ended up in a storage room. He zeroed in on a locked access panel. His steel pincer fingers ripped off the lock, revealing a computer terminal. Opening his mouth, Frenzy emitted a high-intensity shriek.

Suddenly the computer blinked to life! A

message came on the screen: CONNECTING TO PEN-
TAGON NETWORK . . .

Then Frenzy found the file he was trying to
locate: PROJECT ICE MAN: ABOVE TOP SECRET: SECTOR
SEVEN ACCESS ONLY.

Luckily, the Pentagon's computers detected the
foreign signal and immediately alerted Air Force
One. There had been other strange and deadly
attacks in the past few days, and the Pentagon had
been on high alert, looking for anything suspicious.
They had no idea that the Decepticons were
behind the attacks—or that one was aboard Air
Force One.

At that moment, the location of the breach was
discovered.

"Break-in, sector two! Repeat: break-in, sector
two," an agent said into his wrist mic.

Behind the agent, Frenzy shot steel discs from
his chest, and the agent went down.

*Bang!* Another agent fired at Frenzy, but the little Decepticon blocked the bullets. Then he spun
upside down, spitting out more discs.

Before long, more agents dashed into the storage room. They saw the downed men, but no sign
of anyone else. There was just a boom box on the
table playing music. . . .

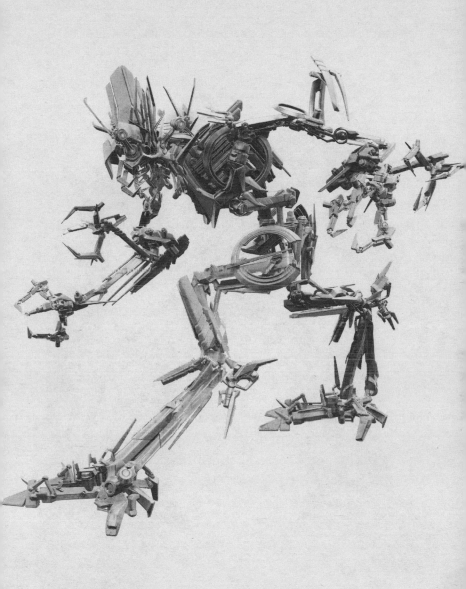

# CHAPTER FOUR

**A**t the Witwicky household, Sam was awakened suddenly from a deep sleep by the sound of his Camaro starting up outside. He looked out the window to see a man with a moustache backing the car out of the driveway.

"Hey! That's my car!" yelled Sam. He threw on clothes and shoes and raced after the car on his bike. He pulled out his cell phone and called 911.

"My car's being stolen," he told the 911 operator. "Get the cops! I'm following him right now."

"Sir, do *not* approach the driver," said the operator. "He could be dangerous."

But Sam wasn't about to let his car get stolen.

He followed the car as the man drove into an old steel yard. Hopping off his bike, Sam watched as the Camaro disappeared into a dense fog. When he finally saw the car again, the mysterious man was gone—and the car was driving itself!

Next, the Camaro began to change shape—and was soon walking on two legs! Sam trembled with shock. He hid behind a crate and watched as the strange machine pulled out a disk that radiated light, which beamed up into space. The light formed the Autobot symbol—Sam recognized it as the same symbol from the steering wheel of the Camaro.

Sam's investigation was cut short by a terrifying sound—vicious barking. He turned to see two Rottweilers coming toward him. Sam ran, jumped onto a stack of crates, and leaped over a barbed-wire fence. The dogs gave chase and bit at his ankle, tripping him.

*Bam!* The Camaro burst through the fence and spun doughnuts around Sam. It honked furiously to hold the dogs away and protect the boy. It worked. Frightened, the dogs ran off.

Sam scrambled backward, away from the car. "Please . . . don't kill me . . ."

Sirens filled the air, and two squad cars drove up.

"Freeze! Hands up!" the sheriff called to Sam.

"Not me! Wrong guy! My car, it's—" began Sam. He pointed toward the Camaro . . . but it was gone.

Down at the police station, Sam tried to explain what he had seen. "Yes, yes. That's what I said. Could I *be* any clearer? It, like, transformed. It stood up!"

"Look, it's been a long night and he's upset," said his father, who had come to pick him up. "I'm taking him home."

The sheriff wasn't convinced at all by Sam's story. But out of obligation, he said, "We'll run it through the wire and see what turns up."

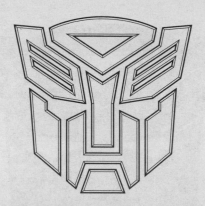

# CHAPTER FIVE

**T**he next morning, Sam woke up and wondered if it had all been a dream. He checked his eBay auction page, but there were no bids. He shuffled to the kitchen and rummaged through the fridge. Sam grabbed the milk, closed the fridge door . . . and screamed. His Camaro was in the driveway.

Stunned, Sam dropped the milk and grabbed the cordless phone. He quickly punched in the number of his best friend.

"Miles, it's me. I thought maybe it was a dream. It's not, it's real. It's alive!"

"Whoa, slow down," said Miles. "What's alive?"

"My car," explained Sam. "It stole itself, it walked, and now it's back. It's trying to kill me! I'm coming over, so don't go anywhere!"

Throwing down the phone, Sam bolted from the house. He grabbed his mother's pink bike and headed toward Miles's neighborhood. He frantically pedaled, looking over his shoulder to see if he was being followed by the Camaro. He was.

Freaking out, Sam raced around a corner and nearly collided with someone walking on the street. He swerved and slammed right into a tree.

"Oh, my god!" said a voice. "Sam, are you okay?"

Feeling dazed, Sam looked up to see the lovely Mikaela Banes looking down at him. Rising to his feet, Sam tried to cover up the aching feeling he had. "Me? Sure, I'm fine."

"Are you hurt?" she asked.

Sam looked down the street and saw the Camaro coming toward him.

"I'm losing my mind," he said. "I've got to go!" Terrified, he grabbed his bike and pedaled off— fast.

Mikaela knew something was wrong. "I'll catch up, okay?" she called out to her friends. Then she unlocked her Vespa and climbed on.

Meanwhile, Sam pedaled across a parking lot. He was constantly looking behind him for the

Camaro, so he never saw the police car that had pulled in front of him. The driver swung his door open.

*Whack!* Sam was knocked off his bike again.

"That hurt!" Sam groaned. "This is like the worst day *ever!*"

Just then, the police car transformed, rising into a sixteen-foot-tall Decepticon named Barricade!

Terrified, Sam ran for his life. Barricade's metal hand swatted Sam into the air, and the boy slammed into a car windshield.

Sam twisted around in pain. "Bad dream, bad dream, please just let me wake up!" he said to himself. He watched in horror as the robot stomped toward him.

"Where are your ancestral artifacts?" demanded Barricade. "Have the Autobots seen the code?"

Scared out of his skull, Sam stammered, "I—I—have n-no idea what you're ta-ta-talking ab-b-out—"

"You will not live to help them," Barricade threatened.

As two giant hands reached for him, Sam jumped off the car and ran. He rounded a corner and collided with Mikaela—again. She and her Vespa went tumbling.

"Ow, my arm!" she cried. "Sam? What's wrong? What's going on?"

"Mikaela, you've got to get up now!" Sam told her, pulling her up.

He did it just in time, for a massive steel foot slammed down on Mikaela's Vespa, crushing it flat. Mikaela looked up at Barricade and screamed. Sam grabbed her hand, and they both ran.

Suddenly another car appeared: the Camaro. Sam watched as the Camaro did a forty-mile-per-hour slide and smashed right into Barricade!

*Maybe the Camaro isn't trying to hurt me,* Sam thought. *Maybe it's trying to protect me.*

The Camaro swung around, honked, and opened its passenger door to Sam and Mikaela. The song "Rescue Me" played loudly from its speakers.

"What's going on?!" asked Mikaela.

Barricade rose from the ground, and the Camaro honked again.

Sam made a decision. "Get in the car," he told Mikaela.

They both dived into the car, and the Camaro peeled out. Transforming back into a police car, Barricade pursued them.

In an abandoned train yard, the Camaro screeched to a stop, its doors flying open. Sam and Mikaela were thrown into the dirt as the Camaro and police car faced off. Swiftly, sections of the

24

Camaro peeled back like a banana, stacking upon itself. It transformed into an Autobot named Bumblebee.

Barricade transformed, too, and the two charged at each other. A section of Barricade's chest opened up, and out sprang Frenzy. The super-thin Decepticon went right for the teens, lashing out at them. Working together, Sam and Mikaela used a power saw to cut him down to size.

"Not so tough without a body, are you?" Sam said to Frenzy, now in pieces on the ground.

Nearby, Barricade flipped Bumblebee onto his back, slamming him down on an aluminum shed. Within no time, the yellow Autobot recovered and transformed his arm into an energy cannon.

*Blast!* The burst of energy hit Barricade directly in the chest, knocking him backward into a construction pit full of spikes. Winding to a stop, Barricade slumped. He had been defeated.

At the top of the ravine where Barricade lay, Frenzy's severed head sprouted tiny legs. Seeing Mikaela's purse just a few feet away, Frenzy crept toward it. He scanned the sleek Sidekick that lay inside. With one quick kick, the real Sidekick went flying and Frenzy climbed inside the purse, reshaping into an exact duplicate.

# CHAPTER SIX

**B**umblebee rolled up to Sam and Mikaela.

"What *is* it?" Mikaela whispered to Sam.

"A robot, I think. But . . . super-advanced," replied Sam. "I don't think he's going to hurt us."

"They just had, like, a droid death match!" Mikaela reminded him.

"I think they want something from me."

"Like what?"

"The other one kept asking about my 'ancestral artifacts' and something about a code," answered Sam. He looked at Bumblebee and asked, "Can you talk?"

Bumblebee turned on the stereo.

"I think he talks through the stereo," Sam said, and applause streamed through the car's speakers.

The Camaro's door swung open.

"I think he wants us to get in," said Sam.

Mikaela was hesitant. "And go where?"

Sam shrugged. "I don't know, but think about it: Fifty years from now when we're looking back on our lives, don't you want to be able to say we had the guts to find out?"

Mikaela considered that for a moment, grabbed her purse, and then hopped in the car.

As they drove, she checked out the shoddy interior. "If you can, like, reshape yourself, why'd you pick such a hoopty? I mean, you could be anything, right?" she asked the Camaro.

Bumblebee's windshield immediately started scanning the streets, searching for the perfect car. Finally, he found it: a brand-new 2007 Chevy Camaro GTO. Beams shot from Bumblebee's headlights, scanning the car's stats to replicate its shape. Before long, Bumblebee's chassis started to reshape, twisting and morphing into an exact duplicate of the GTO.

"Now *this* is a car!" exclaimed Mikaela, as they zoomed off.

On a hilltop, Bumblebee came to a stop and his passengers got out, looking up at the sky. Lights

flickered through the clouds. Suddenly, a burning comet blasted into the atmosphere and broke into pieces. Sam and Mikaela saw the biggest piece crash off in the distance. They hopped back into the Camaro and followed a trail of flaming trees until they came upon a huge ditch off the highway where another comet had landed. However, it wasn't a comet at all . . . it was a thirty-five-foot-tall metallic being.

*Honk!* A horn from an eighteen-wheeler truck blared through the night air. The massive creature turned its face toward the oncoming traffic, scanning the truck. Suddenly, it started reshaping itself into an identical eighteen-wheeler!

The truck drove across the road toward a trembling Sam and Mikaela, its huge grill stopping only inches from them. The eighteen-wheeler transformed into an Autobot, and then leaned down to face them. Its enormous head was ten times bigger than Sam's whole body. He was joined by other vehicles that also transformed themselves. They were all responding to Bumblebee's light signal from the night before.

"I am Optimus Prime," the first Autobot said in a powerful and noble voice.

"Um . . . you speak English?" asked an astonished Mikaela.

"We have assimilated Earth's languages through your World Wide Web," explained Optimus.

"You are aliens?" Sam clarified.

"Correct," replied Optimus. "We are autonomous robotic organisms from the planet Cybertron."

"Autonomous robots . . . *Autobots*," said Mikaela.

Optimus introduced the other Autobots. First was Jazz, Optimus's first lieutenant, who had transformed himself into a sleek Pontiac Solstice.

"Greetings," Jazz said.

Gesturing to the Autobot that had been a pickup truck, Optimus said, "Our weapons specialist: Ironhide."

"This exoskeleton appears suitable for battle," Ironhide said, admiring himself.

"Our medical officer and chief emissary to the High Council of Ancients: Ratchet," Optimus said, pointing to the Autobot that had been a Search and Rescue vehicle. "And you already know Bumblebee, guardian of Sam Witwicky."

"Bumblebee?" said Sam.

"If you can talk, why can't he?" Mikaela asked.

"His vocal processor was destroyed on the battlefields of Tyger Pax," explained Ratchet.

"We come in search of the Allspark—a supreme power that imbues us with the gift of Spark," said Optimus.

"The life force within all Transformers," added Ratchet.

"We must find the Allspark before Megatron does," Optimus said.

Sam was puzzled. "Who's Megatron?"

Optimus paused before he spoke. "Once we were brothers, united. But greed twisted him, and he turned his armies against us. For their betrayal, they bear the name 'Decepticons.'"

Sam and Mikaela exchanged worried looks.

"Megatron feeds on the Sparks of the vanquished, growing stronger with each one he consumes," Optimus continued. "He was the first to follow the Allspark's signal here before succumbing to the ice . . . where your ancestor encountered him."

"The Ice Man!" Sam exclaimed.

"Yes," said Ratchet. "Your great-great-grandfather accidentally triggered Megatron's navigational system, which holds coordinates to the Allspark's location on Earth."

Jazz went on to explain that the beam had blinded Captain Witwicky, but it left a coded imprint on his glasses.

Sam couldn't believe what he was hearing. "The map to the Allspark is on the glasses? But how'd you know all this? Or that I even had them?"

"eBay," answered Ironhide.

"No way!" said Sam, surprised. Suddenly he understood how the Decepticons had found him, too—all his information was right on the Internet, just waiting for them.

"The Allspark calls to us every thousand years," Jazz explained. "We feel its presence here, but cannot trace the exact location. Its signal has been hidden by something."

"If we are first to reach the Allspark, we will return it to our homeworld and rebuild our race," Optimus said.

"And if Megatron finds it?" asked Sam.

Optimus's voice became grave. "He will use it to transform your planet's machinery into a new legion of Decepticons born with a single purpose: conquest of the universe . . . beginning with Earth."

A silence fell over the group as Sam and Mikaela processed what they just heard. Then Mikaela turned to Sam.

"Please tell me you have those glasses!"

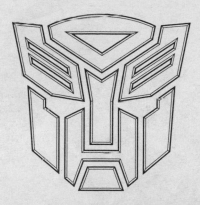

# CHAPTER SEVEN

**B**ack at his house, Sam searched for his great-great-grandfather's glasses. Sneaking through his backyard, the Autobots were trying to hide and stay quiet. They didn't do either well.

Finally Sam found his backpack in the kitchen. As he rifled through it looking for the glasses, Frenzy peered out of Mikaela's purse on the floor. He saw Sam pull the glasses case from his backpack and rose up to strike, but before he could the doorbell rang.

Government agents stood on Sam's front porch. "We need you to come with us," said Simmons, the agent in charge.

Despite protests by Sam's father, the whole Witwicky family—along with Mikaela—was taken into custody in two black SUVs.

Inside the car with Sam and Mikaela, Simmons grilled Sam. "Last night at the station, you told the officer your car 'transformed.' Enlighten me. I need every word."

Sam slipped a hand into his pocket, checking to make sure the glasses were still there. "Listen, this is such a big misunderstanding," he said. "When I said it transformed, I meant that it went from being *my* car to being my *stolen* car. But everything's fine now."

Unfortunately, Simmons wasn't buying it.

Just when Sam thought he'd have to come clean, a giant foot came slamming down on the SUV's hood, crushing it into the pavement. Enormous fingers crashed through the windows and peeled away the roof as if it were the top of an aluminum sardine can.

The Autobots had come to their rescue.

The agents drew their weapons, but as they did, Jazz raised his hand. All of the guns and handcuffs flew magnetically into his palm.

"Gentlemen, let me introduce you to my friend, Optimus Prime," Sam said with a grin.

"Out of the vehicle," ordered Optimus.

37

The agents tumbled from the car. Optimus leaned down and scanned them. "Your nervous systems do not register significant shock. You are not surprised by our existence."

It was true. Sector Seven was a secret branch of the government that had been monitoring and tracking aliens for more than eighty years. Simmons wanted to know more about the Transformers, and that's why he came for Sam.

"Look, uh, there are protocols," Simmons stammered. "I'm not authorized to communicate with you. Except to tell you I can't communicate with you."

The sky filled with Sector Seven choppers cresting the hillside. More SUVs screeched in. Backup had arrived. The Autobots were surrounded.

Combining their efforts, Jazz, Bumblebee, Ratchet, and Ironhide emitted a pulse blast that flattened all the tires on the SUVs. Lifting Sam and Mikaela onto his shoulder, Optimus told them to hold on. He smashed SUVs as he took off.

The helicopters followed, flying under a bridge, in search of Optimus. But he was nowhere to be found. Had he disappeared?

A closer look would have revealed that the Autobot had pressed himself tightly against the underside of the bridge. Sam and Mikaela were

clinging to him . . . until Mikaela began to slip.

"Don't let me go!" she screamed.

"I can't hold on!" Sam yelled.

Bumblebee saw that the teens were in danger. He sped toward the bridge. Unfortunately, as another chopper passed under the bridge, the wind from its whirling blades shook Mikaela and Sam and dislodged their grip. They plummeted down, screaming with fear.

Bumblebee arrived just in time, transformed into a robot, and caught the teens before they hit the ground.

The Autobot set the teens down, not realizing he was now the target of the circling choppers. Firing steel mesh nets, the choppers looped one around Bumblebee's arm and another around his legs.

*"Stop it! You're hurting him!"* screamed Sam. He began to run toward his downed companion, but Simmons held him back.

"Leave him alone!" Sam cried. "He's not going to hurt anyone!"

It was no use. As Sam and Mikaela were taken away, helicopters lifted Bumblebee in the air.

Nearby, the other Autobots watched the terrible scene.

"We have to help Bumblebee," insisted Jazz.

"Negative," replied Optimus. "We cannot engage without harming the humans." He detached himself from the bridge and, with a heavy conscience, reached down to pick up the glasses that had fallen out of Sam's pocket.

# CHAPTER EIGHT

Optimus held Captain Witwicky's glasses up in front of his face. Light beams shot out from his eyes and through the lenses of the glasses, projecting the alien code and pinpointing the Allspark's precise location.

"The Allspark is two hundred and fifty miles from our position," Optimus announced.

But morale was low among the other Autobots.

"They have Bumblebee," Jazz said sadly.

"Bumblebee is a brave soldier who knows the risks of our war." Optimus paused and looked at the destruction around them—crushed cars, broken glass, twisted metal. "If we return the Allspark

to Cybertron, our war will only rage another thousand years. No victors . . . more destruction. More death." The Autobots looked solemn. "If we reach the Allspark first, I will join it with my Spark."

"But you will both be destroyed," Jazz said.

"We will be the last of our kind," Ratchet said.

"I am tired of fighting," Optimus replied, "and our battle now threatens the humans. I must do this alone and you, my true brothers, must carry on."

Then Optimus gave an order: "Autobots: Roll out!"

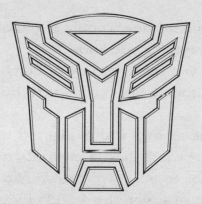

# CHAPTER NINE

**T**hree army Black Hawk helicopters landed at Hoover Dam in Nevada. Along with some top military personnel, Sam and Mikaela were ushered down a walkway. They didn't notice when Frenzy, still in Mikaela's purse, hopped out and scuttled away. The little Decepticon stopped at a sign that read: SECTOR SEVEN ONLY. NO TRESPASSING. Frenzy opened his mouth and emitted a high-pitched scream. He called to his fellow Decepticons: "Sector Seven located. Follow my signal and bring my body." The battle had begun.

\* \* \*

Agent Tom Banachek met Sam and Mikaela at the dam's entrance. "Son, listen to me carefully,"

Banachek said to Sam. "People could die. We need to know everything you know."

But Sam was thinking only of Bumblebee. "Not until you promise me you won't hurt him," he insisted.

Banachek agreed and explained the situation. "We're facing war against a civilization technologically superior to our own. You've had direct contact, which makes you the world's foremost expert on how to beat them."

The group continued down a long, rock tunnel, eventually arriving at a massive underground hangar. Sam and Mikaela looked on in shock. In front of them, a giant Decepticon lay encased in massive blocks of ice. It was Megatron.

Sam found it strange to be looking at the same robot his great-great-grandfather saw more than one hundred years ago. "He's the leader of the Decepticons," said Sam, and explained the difference between the two groups of Transformers.

"They're all looking for something called the Allspark," he continued. Pointing to Megatron, Sam said, "He wants it to transform all our technology and, you know, pretty much take over the universe."

Banachek and Simmons exchanged looks. It didn't take long for Sam to catch on.

"You know where it is," Sam said.

Banachek led everyone inside a top-secret control room. From behind a glass observation deck, Sam and the others saw the Allspark. It gave off a pulsing noise that reverberated throughout the hangar. Tubes and hoses ran from it to consoles, where technicians kept a watchful eye.

Banachek explained that the alien symbols on the Allspark were identical to the ones they pulled from Megatron's data log.

"Yeah," said Sam. "It's a map to the Allspark."

"Oh! That's got to be what they hacked off Air Force One!" said one of the analysts. "They had stolen the data."

Mikaela turned pale as she thought of the Decepticons. "They know it's here."

# CHAPTER TEN

**T**he Decepticons did know the location of the Allspark . . . and they were on their way. Starscream, the F-22 jet, swooped down over Hoover Dam, blasting missiles into a row of power generators. Lights exploded, and the dam shuddered in response.

Suddenly the cryo-blocks containing Megatron began to crack. With an electronic whir, his microchip mind began to wake up.

Aboveground, Blackout, the special ops chopper, roared overhead.

*Kaboom!* Guided missiles caused the dam to explode.

As water showered into the hangar through the cracks in the walls, all of the ice surrounding Megatron began to melt. Soon he had broken free. Transforming into a black hypersonic alien Jet, he blasted through the massive tunnel in search of the Allspark.

The Allspark, however, was still in safe hands. Sam had convinced the Sector Seven agents that the only one who could get the Allspark out of there safely was Bumblebee. The Autobot was released, and he transformed himself back into a Camaro. The Allspark was secured in his backseat, and Sam and Mikaela hopped in front before the car peeled out onto the desert highway.

Back inside a computer lab in the dam, some of the agents and analysts were furiously trying to send out a signal for backup. But it was no use; the Decepticons had cut off all communication. As a last resort, the analysts were trying to use Morse code, when suddenly something slammed at the steel door.

It was Frenzy. Once inside, the Decepticon sent three silver compact discs flying from his chest. They narrowly missed everyone. Struck by a computer keyboard, Frenzy got angry and shot out even more discs. They boomeranged around the room until something unexpected happened: The

discs chopped Frenzy's head right off! But this time, there was no other Decepticon to put him back together.

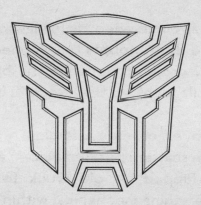

# CHAPTER ELEVEN

**M**egatron had no intention of letting the Autobots escape with the Allspark. As he and the other Decepticons closed in on Bumblebee, Barricade used his police lights to pave his way through the traffic. Bonecrusher's enormous jaws scooped up cars and casually flipped them aside.

As the chase entered the city, Sam, Mikaela, and the others heard an approaching F-22 jet. One of the soldiers sent up a flare as everyone cheered. The Morse code had worked! The jet circled back around, heading straight for the group.

However, Ironhide sensed something was

wrong. "Jazz, Bumblebee: flanking positions!" he ordered, and the Autobots transformed.

The F-22 dropped between the buildings and fired a missile right at the group. The F-22 was Starscream!

*"Mooooove!"* ordered a soldier.

Everyone scattered as Bumblebee and Ironhide lifted and flipped an old truck to shield the humans. Everything mechanical within a one-block range sprouted arms and came alive, causing panic among the people.

Sam ran through the debris to Bumblebee. Seeing that the Autobot's legs had been severed, Sam immediately set about retrieving them. He dragged a leg over, and it started fusing itself back onto Bumblebee's body.

Just then the ground began to tremble. Sam turned to see the tank, Brawl, roll around the corner and flatten two cars.

Two armed Sector Seven vehicles charged and fired. Bent on destruction, Brawl fired back, and the vehicles exploded.

As if Brawl wasn't enough, Bonecrusher wanted in on the action, too. Now Sam and the others were trapped on both ends—by Decepticons.

Brawl transformed, rose up on two legs, and turned his cannon turrets toward the humans.

Just then, Jazz sped in, transformed, and leaped onto Brawl. He wrenched back the Decepticon's arms just as he fired. With a spin kick, Jazz sent him smashing into a building.

Ratchet and Ironhide joined Jazz, and together the three formed a triple threat against Bonecrusher. The soldiers helped out by launching special six-thousand-degree rounds into Bonecrusher's steel construction, causing him to explode from within.

The combined effort worked . . . but the victory was momentary.

Jazz was hit point-blank by an immense pulse blast from . . . Megatron. As Jazz lay on the ground, wounded, Megatron's fury swelled. He plunged his hand into Jazz's chest and pulled out his Spark.

# CHAPTER TWELVE

**O**ptimus arrived just in time to see the violent act. Optimus charged in to face his nemesis. "Megatron," he said.

Megatron shook his head in disgust. "Pathetic . . . You still make allies of the weak."

"Where you see weakness, I see strength," Optimus said.

"So be it, brother," replied Megatron. "Our war begins again . . . on Earth."

As the Transformers charged at each other, Bumblebee urgently grabbed Sam's hand. Into his palm, he placed the Allspark.

"No! I'm not going to leave you," Sam told him.

Bumblebee opened his mouth and painfully

managed to utter, "Goooo, Saamm."

As army Black Hawk helicopters flew past, one of the soldiers on the ground handed Sam a flare. "Get to that roof and signal the chopper. We'll cover you," he said.

"But—what am I supposed to—"

"Time to see what you're made of, soldier! Get the Allspark out of the city, as far as you can, or a lot of people are going to die!"

Sam looked to Mikaela for guidance.

"No matter what happens," she said. "I'm glad I got in the car with you."

Sam smiled before he ran off into a nearby abandoned building. He bolted up the main stairs toward the roof.

*Bam!* Megatron's head smashed through the floors below him. Five gigantic fingers rose, reaching for Sam and swatting away the stairs beneath his feet. When he finally reached the roof, there was not much left of the building. Sam was trapped on a small patch of cement when Megatron finally cornered him.

"Give me the Allspark, boy," demanded the Decepticon. "You aren't strong enough to defy me!"

But Sam clung valiantly to the Allspark. "No," he said, trying his best to mask his fright.

"I see the fear in your eyes," Megatron said. "You can end it . . . or you *will* die."

Sam's face grew determined. He knew this was the most important moment of his life. "I AM *NEVER* GIVING IT TO YOU!"

Enraged, Megatron fired at Sam, blowing out the rooftop beneath him. Sam tumbled and fell through the air!

Optimus, who was stretched between two buildings, lunged for him. Thankfully, Sam landed on Optimus's chest. The only problem now was that Sam and Optimus were *both* falling. Megatron hurtled down from above, like an eagle plunging in for the kill.

Optimus cupped Sam protectively against his chest, and used his other hand to rip through the building frame to slow their fall. They finally landed with a huge impact.

As the dust cleared, Optimus's fingers slowly opened to reveal Sam, dazed but safe.

"You would give your own life to protect the Allspark?" asked Optimus.

Sam thought of a phrase his father often said, and offered Optimus the Allspark. "No sacrifice, no victory."

The Autobot understood, but before he could take the Allspark, Optimus was hammered with

pulse blasts from Blackout and Starscream.

Then Megatron plunged down, shouting, "It's mine! The Allspark is mine!" He towered above Sam, ready to crush him.

Wounded but headstrong, Optimus called to Sam. "Use the Allspark, Sam! Aim for his Spark!"

Sam mustered up all his courage and slammed the Allspark straight into Megatron's chest. With a blinding flash, Megatron's Spark exploded. Lightning burst out and energy swirled around as all of Megatron's life force was released.

The battle was over.

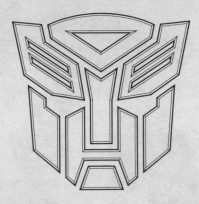

# CHAPTER THIRTEEN

**B**lackout and Brawl died in battle. The military had taken out Barricade, and Bonecrusher was reduced to a pile of metal. The only Decepticon left was Starscream. Realizing he was outnumbered, the F-22 jet flew off.

From the wreckage, Mikaela and Bumblebee emerged. Sam was relieved to see that they were both unharmed.

Ratchet and Ironhide carried the lifeless body of Jazz, gently setting him down in front of Optimus.

Sam turned to Optimus. How would the Autobots survive now? "Without the Allspark,

you're the last of your kind."

Optimus kneeled down to Jazz. "We will survive. We must," he said. "For those who did not."

"Look!" Mikaela said suddenly, as she approached the edge of a cliff.

Everyone joined her. Deep inside a giant crater was Megatron's body, covered in rubble. The light in his eyes dimmed and then went out. Optimus bowed his head.

"You left me no choice . . . brother," he said softly.

He stood proudly next to Sam and Mikaela. They were together, humans and Autobots, united in the battle against evil.

After that momentous day, life was definitely different for Sam. He had a new confidence and a sense of pride that he had done the right thing—and helped save Earth in the process. He was sure his great-great-grandfather would have been proud.

Monday morning at school, Sam was talking in the hallway to Miles between classes. He looked up to see Mikaela heading his way with her friends. But Mikaela looked only at her boyfriend, Trent, who was standing in front of Sam.

*Oh, well,* Sam thought. *I guess some things don't ever change.*

But Mikaela passed right by Trent. She walked up to Sam instead! Sam started to say something, but Mikaela didn't give him a chance. She planted a kiss on his lips—right there in front of everyone. It turned out that saving the world did have some perks!

Meanwhile, Optimus and the remaining Autobots were also adjusting to their new life. Even though the Decepticons were vanquished, the Autobots had no planet to return to. Now that they had proved themselves to be allies to humans, they made a new home on Earth. Hiding in plain sight, they lived among the people.

Optimus Prime was hopeful that the peaceful partnership between the Autobots and the humans would continue. He wondered about other existing Autobots, lost in space.

Standing on top of Mount Everest, Optimus called out to them. "I send this message to all surviving Autobots taking refuge among the stars! You are not alone. We are here," he said. "We are waiting."